E PSK
Hat    Hatay, Nona.
       Charlie's ABC

MW00910919

## DATE DUE

| | | | |
|---|---|---|---|
| | | | |
| | | | |
| | | | |
| | | | |
| | | | |
| | | | |
| | | | |
| | | | |
| | | | |
| | | | |
| | | | |
| | | | |

# Charlie's ABC

Text and photographs © 1993 by Nona Hatay.
All rights reserved. Printed in Singapore.
For information address Hyperion Books for Children,
114 Fifth Avenue, New York, New York 10011.

FIRST EDITION
1  3  5  7  9  10  8  6  4  2

Library of Congress Cataloging-in-Publication Data
Hatay, Nona.
Charlie's ABC / Nona Hatay — 1st ed.   p.   cm.
Summary: Photographs illustrate some of
the common things in the life of a young child,
from A (alphabet) to Z (zipper).
ISBN 1-56282-352-3 (trade) — ISBN 1-56282-353-1 (lib. ed.)
1. English language — Alphabet — Juvenile literature.
[1. Alphabet.]   I. Title.   PE1155.H38   1993
[E] — dc20   92-72030   CIP   AC

The artwork for each picture is prepared
using black-and-white photographs,
hand colored with crayons.
This book is set in 72-point Futura Bold.
Book design by Joann Hill Lovinski.

# Charlie's ABC

## Nona Hatay

**Hyperion Books for Children    New York**

**For my beloved daughter,**

Charlie's sister**, Heidi Merris**

alphabet

ball

# chairs

# dog

eyes

# flowers

gloves

hat

ice cream

jam

**kite**

lion

mirror

necklace

**oranges**

pictures

quilt

# rug

sweater

teddy bear

**umbrella**

vegetables

**water**

xylophone

**yarn**

zipper